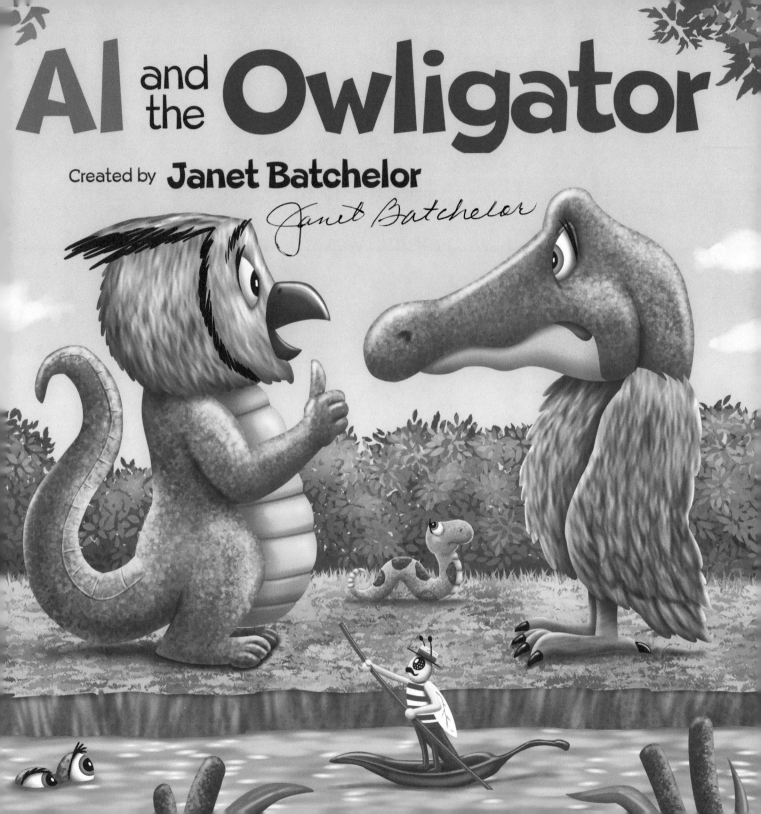

To our **children**

For our **grandchildren**

and **great grandchildren**

With thanks to my **husband**,

In loving memory of our **mothers**

Al and the Owligator

Created by **Janet Batchelor**

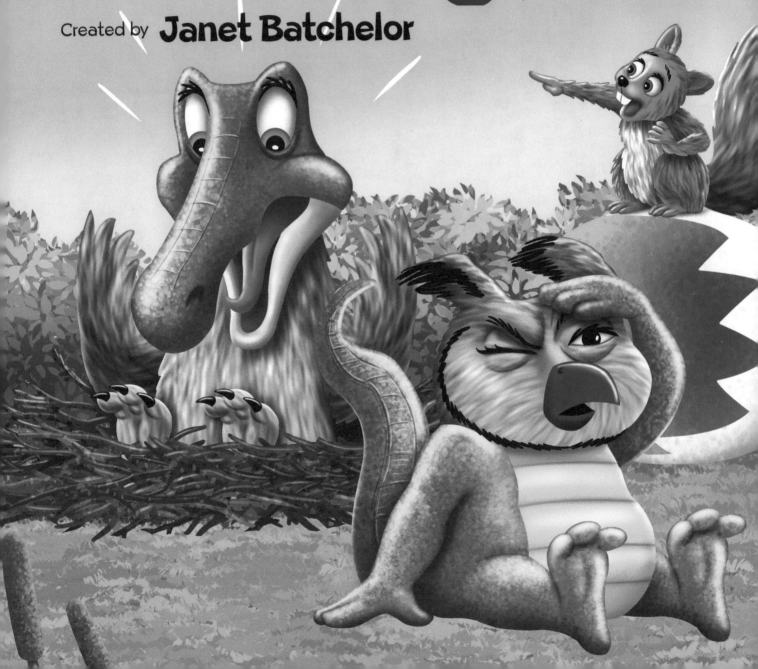

The little owl inside the egg
was tossing in his sleep.

His nest was high above the ground,
up where the willows weep.

He'd grown so much inside the egg,
he didn't fit at all.

It felt a lot like trying to wear a coat
that's much too small.

He tossed and turned, but as he did,
his egg rolled left and right.

And soon it moved too near the edge
and rolled right out of sight!

An alligator nest
was in the grass
beneath the tree.

The baby 'gator in the egg heard
someone shouting "WHEEEEE!"

And then the little 'gator felt a
crash against his shell.

He thought it came from up above,
but it was hard to tell.

The owl and alligator eggs had scrambled just a bit.

But the eggshells fell right into place and made a perfect fit.

Morning brought the sunshine.
It was time to play outside.

The little ones were ready now to
push the egg aside.

They put their feet together and
their backs against the shell.

And when they shoved with all their might,
the egg halves quickly fell.

The round owl eyes were squinting
for the sunlight was so bright.

But the alligator eyes could see
that things were not quite right.

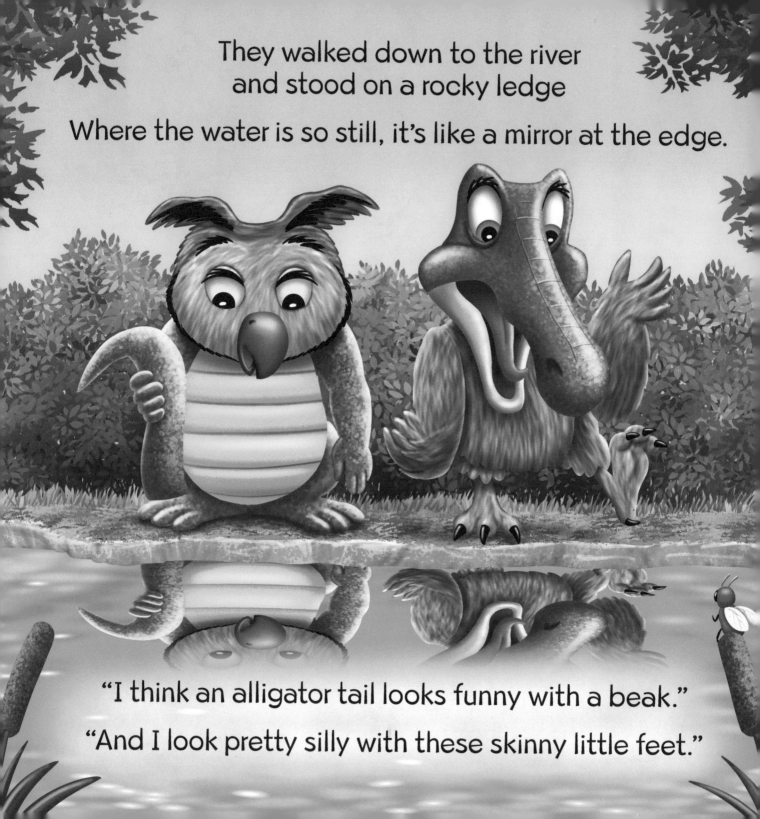

They walked down to the river
and stood on a rocky ledge

Where the water is so still, it's like a mirror at the edge.

"I think an alligator tail looks funny with a beak."

"And I look pretty silly with these skinny little feet."

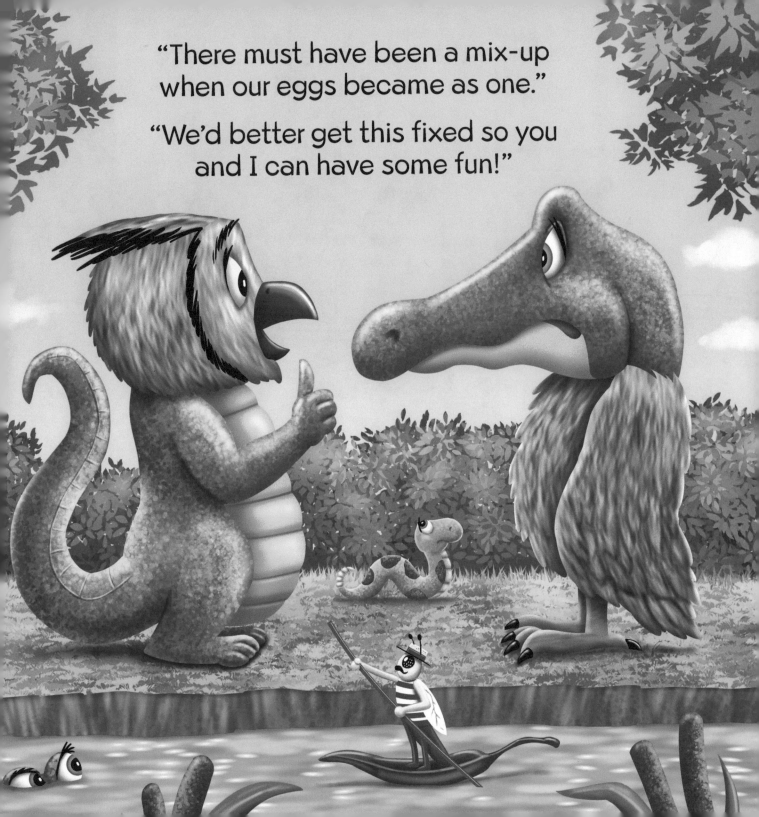

"I know they're in here somewhere,"
Al said, searching in his nest.

He found two safety helmets that
were perfect for the test.

"And you'll have owl wings again
to match your owl eyes.

And I will have my lovely tail and
feet that are my size."

Flying looked so easy,
but it wasn't, Al found out.

He flapped and jumped and jumped
and flapped and fluttered all about.

"You're flying!" Al heard Owligator shouting up to him.

Before he knew what happened, his owl feet were on a limb.

Then Owligator used his tail
to clear the perfect site:

Right underneath the limb where
Al was resting from his flight.

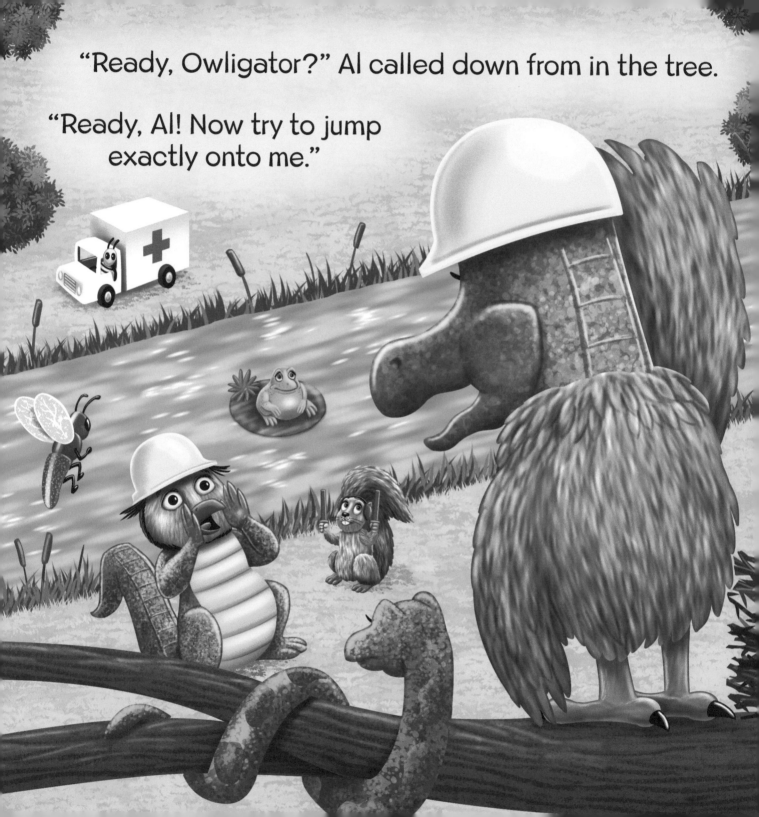

"Ready, Owligator?" Al called down from in the tree.

"Ready, Al! Now try to jump exactly onto me."

"Here I come!" Al closed his eyes
and sailed down from the limb.

"Hooray!" said Owligator.
Al had landed right on him!

"Are you all right, Owligator?"

"Yes! And you can call me Owl.
We did it, Alligator!
I am now a full-fledged fowl!"

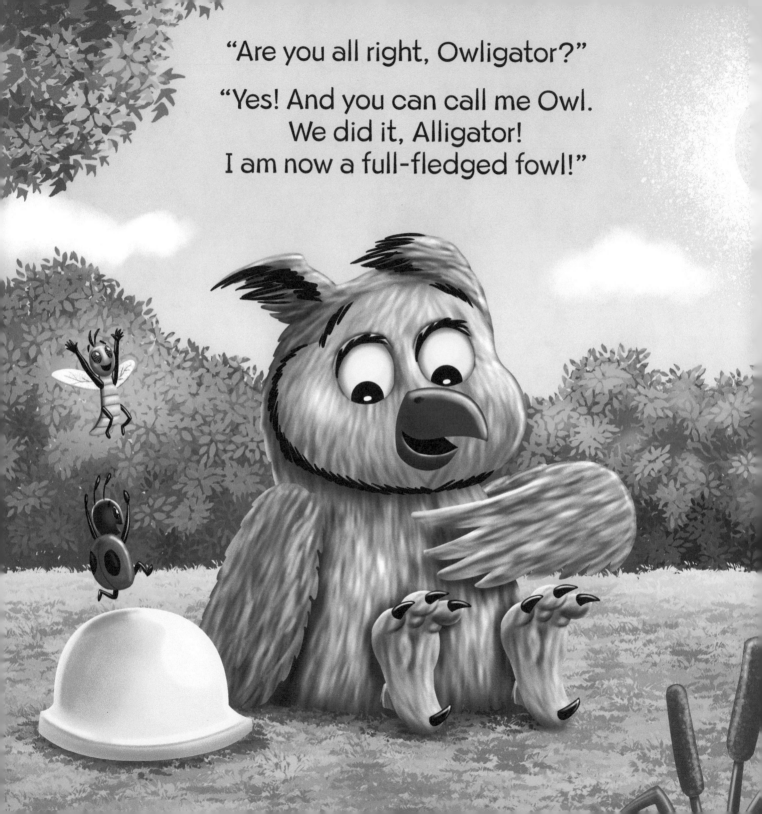

"And I'm an alligator with a tail to match my snout.

I'm glad we worked together, Owl, to figure all this out."

"Just because we're different doesn't mean we can't be friends."

"Let's meet again tomorrow and have fun that never ends."